PUFFIN BOOKS

MR MAJEIKA AND THE SCHOOL BOOK WEEK

Humphrey Carpenter (1946–2005), the author and creator of *Mr Majeika*, was born and educated in Oxford. He went to a school called the Dragon School where exciting things often happened and there were some very odd teachers – you could even call it magical! He became a full-time writer in 1975 and was the author of many award-winning biographies. As well as the *Mr Majeika* titles, his children's books also included *Shakespeare Without the Boring Bits* and *More Shakespeare Without the Boring Bits*. He wrote plays for radio and theatre and founded the children's drama group The Mushy Pea Theatre Company. He played the tuba, double bass, bass saxophone and keyboard.

Humphrey once said, "The nice thing about being a write─ ─h─t ─o─ can make magic happen witho─ ──── ─── ── are the only tricks yo─ ─── ─── ── floated up to the ceili── ── ── ── ─ e out of his pocket, gr── ── ── y.' And you will believe that it really happened! That's magic, isn't it?"

Books by Humphrey Carpenter

MR MAJEIKA

MR MAJEIKA AND THE DINNER LADY

MR MAJEIKA AND THE GHOST TRAIN

MR MAJEIKA AND THE HAUNTED HOTEL

MR MAJEIKA AND THE LOST SPELL BOOK

MR MAJEIKA AND THE MUSIC TEACHER

MR MAJEIKA AND THE SCHOOL BOOK WEEK

MR MAJEIKA AND THE SCHOOL CARETAKER

MR MAJEIKA AND THE SCHOOL INSPECTOR

MR MAJEIKA AND THE SCHOOL PLAY

MR MAJEIKA AND THE SCHOOL TRIP

MR MAJEIKA ON THE INTERNET

MR MAJEIKA VANISHES

THE PUFFIN BOOK OF CLASSIC

CHILDREN'S STORIES (Ed.)

SHAKESPEARE WITHOUT THE BORING BITS

MORE SHAKESPEARE WITHOUT THE

BORING BITS

Humphrey Carpenter

Mr Majeika and the School Book Week

Illustrated by Frank Rodgers

PUFFIN

PUFFIN BOOKS

Published by the Penguin Group
Penguin Books Ltd, 80 Strand, London WC2R 0RL, England
Penguin Group (USA), Inc., 375 Hudson Street, New York, New York 10014, USA
Penguin Books Australia Ltd, 250 Camberwell Road, Camberwell,
Victoria 3124, Australia
Penguin Books Canada Ltd, 10 Alcorn Avenue, Toronto, Ontario, Canada M4V 3B2
Penguin Books India (P) Ltd, 11 Community Centre, Panchsheel Park,
New Delhi – 110 017, India
Penguin Books (NZ) Ltd, Cnr Rosedale and Airborne Roads, Albany, Auckland,
New Zealand
Penguin Books (South Africa) (Pty) Ltd, 24 Sturdee Avenue, Rosebank 2196, South Africa

Penguin Books Ltd, Registered Offices: 80 Strand, London WC2R 0RL, England

www.penguin.com

First published by Viking 1992
Published in Puffin Books 1993
001

Text copyright © Humphrey Carpenter, 1992
Illustrations copyright © Frank Rodgers, 1992
All rights reserved

The moral right of the author and illustrator has been asserted

Set in Palatino

Made and printed in England by Clays Ltd, St Ives plc

British Library Cataloguing in Publication Data
A CIP catalogue record for this book is available from the British Library

ISBN-13: 978-0-141-34702-8

www.greenpenguin.co.uk

MIX
Paper from
responsible sources
FSC™ C018179

Penguin Books is committed to a sustainable
future for our business, our readers and our planet.
This book is made from Forest Stewardship
Council™ certified paper.

ALWAYS LEARNING   **PEARSON**

Contents

1. *Fight the Flab*

"This term," said Mr Potter, the head teacher, addressing the first assembly of the new term at St Barty's School, "we have a new games teacher. Her name is Miss Johnson, and she'll be joining us next week. She would have been here today, but she's suffering from the flu."

"Huh, some games teacher if she goes to bed with the flu," shouted Hamish Bigmore, from the back of the hall. "You never get ill if you're really fit – like me!" Hamish, the nuisance of Class Three, had been spending the holidays taking a body-building course. He had brought his chest-expander to school, and was doing exercises with it in assembly.

"Be quiet, Hamish," called Mr Potter,
"and put that thing away."

Hamish paid no attention. "I was once a
five-stone weakling," he crowed, "but look
at me now."

"Yes," said Thomas, who was standing next to him, "look at him now. He's an eight-stone weakling. The only exercise Hamish ever takes is munching chocolates!"

"He must have the strongest jaw in the school," said Thomas's twin brother, Pete. "But as for the rest of him, he looks like a bungled entry for a Stuff-a-Cushion competition."

"I'll have you know," snarled Hamish, "that my mum takes me to her Weightwatchers class to show me off."

"Yes," said Jody, Thomas and Pete's friend. "To show you off as an awful warning."

Hamish made a very loud, very rude noise at Thomas, Pete and Jody, and Mr Potter got very angry and gave them all detention during the lunch break.

The following Monday morning, Mr Potter was sitting in his office, trying to add up the dinner money, when the door burst open. "Are you Potter?" boomed a voice. "Pringle's the name, Prudence Pringle. I'm your new games teacher."

Mr Potter blinked. "But we were expecting a Miss Johnson," he said.

"The poor thing's really very ill with the flu," thundered Miss Pringle, "so she sent me instead. Shake!" She offered Mr Potter her hand, and when he took it, he found his arm being almost shaken off.

"But I d-d-don't know anything about you, Miss, er, Pringle," he stuttered. "What are your qualifications?"

"Pretty good," snapped Miss Pringle, releasing Mr Potter's hand. "Just back from training the British team for the Olympics."

"Training them in what?" asked Mr Potter.

"Oh, everything – running, jumping, throwing things, the greasy pole, you name it and I'm a gold medallist in it."

"Er, I see," said Mr Potter, who didn't remember seeing a greasy pole competition when he had watched the Olympic Games on T V. "But if you're so fit, Miss Pringle, why is your face wrapped up in a scarf?" For Miss Pringle's mouth and the end of her nose were entirely hidden by a long scarf.

"None of your business," snapped Miss Pringle, in a rather different voice from the booming one in which she had spoken so far – a voice which Mr Potter thought he

had heard somewhere before, though he
couldn't remember where.

"Perhaps you've got toothache?" he
suggested nervously.

"That's right," said Miss Pringle,

returning to the low-pitched voice. "I've got toothache. And now, Potter, I'm going to get on with the job. I want the whole school out in the playground, *now*."

"The whole school?" queried Mr Potter. "But we don't organize games and P E like that at St Barty's. We do it class by class. I'll show you the timetable."

"I said the *whole* school," boomed Miss Pringle, picking up Mr Potter by the scruff of the neck. "The whole school, *including the teachers*!"

Meanwhile, Mr Majeika was teaching Class Three. Mr Majeika had once been a wizard. Occasionally he forgot that he wasn't a wizard any more, and did some magic. But most of the time there was no magic in Class Three, just ordinary lessons, some of them interesting, but

many of them rather boring. There was a boring one going on now. So nobody, not even Mr Majeika (who was bored by the lesson himself), minded when Mr Potter stuck his head round the door of Class

Three, and explained that the new games teacher wished to have the whole school out in the playground right away.

"So sorry to interrupt you, Majeika," said Mr Potter, "but Miss Pringle insists. She's rather a forceful lady."

"Not at all, Mr Potter," said Mr Majeika. "I don't mind having a little break from teaching. I'll see Class Three back here, shall I, in about half an hour?"

"I'm afraid you've got to come too, Majeika," said Mr Potter. "She wants the teachers as well."

When Mr Majeika and Class Three reached the playground, Miss Pringle was already roaring out orders to the other classes. "*Run* on the spot, *at* the double! One–two, one–two, one–*two*! I can see three teachers *slacking* at the back there. No laziness, or I'll have you all doing extra PE after school." The teachers muttered and complained, but Miss Pringle ran up behind them, blowing her whistle, and bullied them into running on the spot as fast as the pupils.

When Miss Pringle saw Class Three arriving, she made them stand in the middle of the playground, where everyone could see them. "Ah," she boomed, "Class Three. Rather late, aren't we? Let's have you all touching your toes twenty times, starting *now*!" She blew her whistle, and walked up and down the line as they all touched their toes, shouting at anyone who wasn't doing it properly – anyone, that is, except Hamish Bigmore.

Hamish was only half-pretending to bend over. He was taking chocolates out of

his pocket and stuffing them into his mouth. Thomas and Pete expected that Miss Pringle would get in a rage with him when she saw this, but instead she said: "Well done, Hamish! Aren't you a good boy?" Then she turned to Mr Majeika. "As for you, Majeika," she roared, "put your back into it! Just because you call yourself a teacher, that doesn't mean you can slack. Come out to the front and do twenty press-ups!"

Poor Mr Majeika protested, but Mr Potter called out, "You'd better do as she says, Majeika. She insists that the entire school trains to Olympic standards."

"That's right, Potter," boomed Miss Pringle. "And that goes for you too. You can do *forty* press-ups, starting right away."

Half an hour later, utterly exhausted, Class Three staggered back into their classroom. Mr Majeika was panting for breath. "If this goes on," he gasped, "I'm going to have to find another job. I can't stay here if Mr Potter's going to allow her to be in charge."

"Did you notice something funny, Mr

Majeika?" asked Jody. "She knew Hamish's name, and yours, but she's only just arrived in the school."

"And she didn't mind Hamish eating chocolates," said Pete. "Something odd is going on."

"Why has she got that scarf wrapped round her face?" asked Thomas.

"Mr Potter says it's because she's got toothache," said Mr Majeika.

"She reminds me of someone," said Jody, "but I can't think who. I'm sure there's something fishy about her."

"Fishy or not," said Mr Majeika, "I just wish she'd go away."

But she didn't. Miss Pringle was definitely at St Barty's to stay, and as the days passed, she made the children and teachers do more and more exhausting exercises. "Why does Mr Potter put up with it?" asked Jody. "She's exhausting him as much as any of us – she made him do fifty press-ups today."

"He's terrified of her," said Thomas. "I saw her pick him up with one hand and shake him. He doesn't stand a chance."

"And meanwhile, Hamish just stands there stuffing chocolates, and she doesn't care," said Pete. "I don't understand it. For some reason he's her star pupil. I can't make out –" He stopped. "Wait a minute," he said. "Star Pupil. Doesn't that ring a bell?"

"Wilhelmina Worlock," said Mr Majeika. "You don't think . . . ?"

Wilhelmina Worlock was a witch, and a very nasty one. She had come to St Barty's as a music teacher, and had tried to take

over the school. The only person to whom
she hadn't been horrible was Hamish
Bigmore, whom she called her Star Pupil.
Mr Majeika had managed to get rid of her
by magic, but since then she had turned
up several times, trying to get her revenge.

"It can't be Miss Worlock," said Thomas.
"She hasn't got glasses."

"She could have taken them off, you fat-head," said Pete. "Pull that scarf off her face, Mr Majeika, and see if it really is her."

Mr Majeika thought for a moment. "Maybe you're right," he said. "But if it is Wilhelmina, she could be very dangerous. Even if I try spells against her, I could have an awful time, because she can use magic back at me."

"Yes, Mr Majeika," said Jody, "do be careful. You know how dangerous she is."

The next day, Thomas hurried into Class Three. "I'm sure it's her," he said. "I caught a glimpse of her winding the scarf around her face as she was coming out of the staff cloakroom, and the nose and chin looked just like Miss Worlock. And she was tucking some glasses into her pocket."

"And she's put up a notice," said Jody, "announcing that there's to be an Olympic Sports Day, at which the whole school will compete for the title of Star Pupil."

"She'll want Hamish to win, of course," said Pete.

"I can't think how she'll manage that," said Thomas. "Hamish has eaten so many chocolates this term that he can scarcely walk, let alone run, jump, pole-vault, throw the discus, or do all the other Olympic sports."

The Olympic Sports Day dawned bright and clear, and lots of parents gathered on the school sports field to watch the competitions.

"Hello, boys and girls, mums and dads," announced Miss Pringle, through a megaphone. "Welcome to our Olympic Sports Day. We'll begin with the long jump."

Everyone lined up to take their turn at the long jump. Miss Pringle stood by the jump, blowing her whistle for each competitor, and writing down how far they had jumped. Finally, there was only Hamish left to do the jump. "What a feeble lot you are," roared Miss Pringle.

"We're not feeble," shouted Thomas angrily. "We've most of us jumped pretty well."

"Quiet, there, cheeky monkey, or I'll make you do a hundred press-ups. And now it's the turn of Hamish Bigmore." Miss Pringle smiled sweetly at Hamish.

Hamish grinned a sticky grin back at her – his face was smeared with chocolate –

and waddled up towards the jump. "Look at that," giggled Jody. "He won't be able to jump at all." But as Hamish reached the line, Miss Pringle pointed a finger at the long jump, and the ground itself suddenly *shrank*, so that Hamish only had to step over the line to reach the end of the sand-pit.

"A record!" screamed Miss Pringle at the top of her voice. "Hamish Bigmore has broken an Olympic record!" She waved her hands again, and the ground stretched out again to its normal length, so that Hamish was at the far end of the sand-pit.

"What a barefaced pair of cheats they are," fumed Pete. "Surely all the parents saw what happened?"

"It was magic," said Mr Majeika, "and they don't believe in magic, so they must think they imagined it." Certainly there were some puzzled faces among the parents. They looked as if they didn't believe their eyes.

"High jump!" announced Miss Pringle, and lined everyone up behind the high jump. Again, Hamish was left till last, and when his turn came, Miss Pringle called out, "And now for our record-breaking Hamish Bigmore. Let's see if you can break another Olympic record, Hamish." She raised the bar to a much higher level than it had been before.

"He'll never get over that," laughed Thomas.

"Can't you guess what's going to happen?" said Jody.

Sure enough, when Hamish ran up to the bar, Miss Pringle pointed her finger at it, and in a fraction of a second it had dropped to ground level – and then, when Hamish was safely over, it rose to its full height again.

"Another record!" she screamed. "Hamish Bigmore is a world-beater. No need to go on with the Sports Day, because Hamish Bigmore is definitely the

Star Pupil of St Barty's! *But it isn't St Barty's
any more.*" She unwound the scarf from her
face, and put on her glasses. "No, my
dears, it's the Wilhelmina Worlock
Olympic Sports School, where we do
press-ups all day long, the parents as well
as the children, and anyone who doesn't
manage to touch their toes a hundred

times will be *turned into a toad*! He, he, he, he, he!"

"Wait a minute," called Mr Majeika. "Now that you've revealed yourself, Wilhelmina, as the wicked witch you really are, do you admit that you and Hamish are the biggest cheats that have ever been seen on a school sports field?"

"Certainly not, you weasly little wizard," snapped Miss Worlock. "Hamish would earn a gold medal in any Olympic sport, and what's more, so would I."

"Very well," said Mr Majeika. "Show us. If you're so brilliant, why doesn't Hamish try the long jump and the high jump again – with *you* competing as well?"

Miss Worlock scowled at him, but Hamish said, "Of course we will! We'll show you who are the record-breakers."

Unwillingly, Miss Worlock lined up alongside Hamish for the long jump. "Go!" shouted Mr Majeika, and they ran and jumped – and landed with a muddy splash, because Mr Majeika had waved his hands and turned the sand-pit into a mess of sticky mud.

"Why, you –" spluttered Miss Worlock, as she got to her feet and tried to scrape off the mud. "I'll turn you into a –"

"The high jump first, Wilhelmina," said Mr Majeika. "Let's see if you and Hamish can get over that bar without magical assistance."

Grumbling that she would turn him into a toad, or worse, as soon as she'd finished the high jump, Miss Worlock again lined up with Hamish.

"Go!" shouted Mr Majeika, and the two of them ran and jumped.

They both crashed straight into the bar – and suddenly, out of nowhere (because Mr Majeika had waved his hands again), there was a bucket of water on top of the bar, which tipped all over Hamish and Miss Worlock.

"Right!" yelled Miss Worlock. "I'm not just going to turn you into a toad, Majeika. I'm going to make you into scrambled egg

and have you for breakfast. I'm going to –"

"I've got a better suggestion, Wilhelmina," interrupted Mr Majeika. "Why not throw that discus at me? It ought to knock me for six – except that you're not strong enough to chuck it even a few inches." He pointed to a heavy, round discus that Miss Worlock had brought with her to the Sports Day.

"If it hits you, it'll hurt you badly, Mr Majeika," said Thomas anxiously.

"Ssh," whispered Mr Majeika.

"Not strong enough, eh?" roared Miss Worlock. "I'll show you, you little wimp of a wizard. I'll chuck that discus so hard, it'll knock you into the twenty-second century. Just watch!" And she picked up the discus.

"If you were a *really* powerful witch," said Mr Majeika, "you'd spin round and round before throwing it, to make it fly at about a hundred miles an hour. But *you* wouldn't be able to do that."

"Oh, wouldn't I?" sneered Miss Worlock. "You just watch!" And she began to spin round, faster and faster. "Here it comes," she called.

But Mr Majeika had waved his hands,

and something seemed to be wrong with
Wilhelmina Worlock. The discus did not
leave her hand, but it seemed to be stuck
to her. And she was turning faster and
faster, until she became just a blur.

Suddenly there was a roaring sound.
She had spun so fast that she had drilled a

hole in the ground, which was opening up beneath her. She gave a shriek of rage – "I'll get you, Majeika!" – but there was nothing she could do to save herself. In a moment, she had vanished, and there was silence.

Everyone crowded round the hole and

looked into it. "It goes a long way down, Mr Majeika," said Jody.

"Yes," said Mr Majeika, "probably as far as Australia. We shan't be seeing her again for some time, I think. She can find herself a job training Australians for the Olympic Games. As for you, Hamish Bigmore, when you've washed off that mud, you'd better do some press-ups. The only gold medal you'd stand any chance of winning looking like that would be for chocolate-eating."

2. *Story Time*

Each term, a different class at St Barty's took it in turns to look after the school library. Last term it had been Class Four, and they had left everything very tidy. All the books were in the right place, and the cards which showed who had borrowed what had been neatly filled in. They had made the library look bright and cheerful by putting up posters of famous authors.

This term it was Class Three's turn. Mr Majeika organized a rota, so that groups of four people at a time were on library duty for a week. Being on library duty meant that you had to check that all the books were returned on time by the people who had borrowed them. You also had to keep everything neat and orderly.

Thomas, Pete and Jody were put on library duty with Hamish Bigmore. "That's not fair, Mr Majeika," said Thomas. "You know what Hamish is like. He'll muck everything up."

Mr Majeika sighed. "He's got to be in somebody's group," he said, "and you

three are tough enough to stand up to him."

Pete and Thomas were rather flattered by this, but Jody said, "It's no use being tough. What we need with Hamish is eyes in the back of our heads. The moment we turn our backs, he'll be up to something."

As it happened, the week in which Thomas, Pete, Jody and Hamish were on library duty was going to be rather a special one. St Barty's was holding a Book Week, and on the last day a children's author was coming to St Barty's to talk to the school. Her name was Penelope Primrose, and she was well known for her picture books for very young children. They were about a rabbit called Little Bluebell.

"Yuck," said Pete, when he heard that

she was coming to St Barty's. "Why do we have to have *her*?"

"Never mind," said Mr Majeika. "I'm sure it will be very interesting to hear how books are made. Now, mind you keep the library nice and tidy all week, but especially on Friday, when Penelope Primrose is visiting."

All week long, Thomas, Pete and Jody put away books, filled out borrowers' cards, straightened chairs and tables, and made sure there were displays of books for everyone to see. Much to their surprise, Hamish Bigmore actually helped them, with a friendly smile on his face.

At first, Thomas was suspicious. "Hamish must be up to something," he said. "It's just not like him to do a job like this without complaining."

"I agree," said Pete. "There's definitely some trickery up Hamish's sleeve."

But Jody said, "I wish people would give Hamish a chance. People always expect him to behave badly, so of course he does. If someone encouraged him for a change, he might become a reformed character. Well done, Hamish!" she called out to Hamish, who had got some polish and a duster from one of the cleaning ladies, and was polishing a table.

"Thank you, Jody," said Hamish. "I'm glad there's someone who doesn't always think the worst of me."

"There you are," whispered Jody to Thomas and Pete. "What did I tell you? You've been hurting his feelings with all your remarks. Can't you see that, for once, he's really trying his best?"

Shamefaced, Thomas and Pete got on with their work.

On Friday morning, the day of Penelope Primrose's visit, the library was looking spick and span. There were vases of flowers on the tables, and a big poster of Penelope Primrose had been put up. All

her books were displayed on a table. She was going to come and talk to Class Three at the end of the morning. Her talks to the other classes would be given in their own classrooms, but she had said she wanted to see the school library, and as Class Three were on library duty, it was decided that she should meet them in the library itself.

At the beginning of the mid-morning break, Jody popped into the library to make sure everything was ready. It all looked very nice. When the bell rang, she went to Class Three's classroom for the lesson before Penelope Primrose's talk.

"Where's Hamish Bigmore?" asked Mr Majeika when the lesson began.

"He said he was feeling sick, Mr Majeika," said Pandora. "He's gone to lie down in the medical room."

It crossed Jody's mind that, as the medical room was next door to the library, it would be really easy for Hamish Bigmore to get up to mischief and spoil all their preparations for Penelope Primrose's visit. But she felt that, after all she had been saying to Thomas and Pete about how they should trust Hamish, she shouldn't be expecting the worst of him like this.

When the bell rang for the end of the lesson, Mr Majeika said, "Now, will you all please go to the library, and I'll go and fetch Penelope Primrose and take her there to meet you." So off they all trooped.

Mr Majeika went to the staff room, where Penelope Primrose was drinking a glass of orange juice and talking to Mr Potter. "How do you do?" she said to Mr Majeika. "I told Mr Potter that I *never* drink

strong grown-up drinks like coffee or tea.
I'm just a little girlie at heart, and I like a
little glass of milkie and a chockie bickie, or
a little squeezie of orange juice. Oh, I have
had *such* a sweet time this morning with all
the little tiny tots. They *do* love my
bookies! And have you got more little
babes for me to meet, Mr Majeika?"

"Er, yes," said Mr Majeika, wondering what Class Three would make of Penelope Primrose. "Come this way, please." And he led her to the school library.

There seemed to be some sort of disturbance going on. Mr Majeika could hear Jody shouting at Hamish. But when he opened the door and took Penelope Primrose in, there was a sudden hush. "Here we are, everyone," he said. "Here's Penelope Primrose to talk to you." He led her to a chair beside the table which was piled with her books.

"Hello, kiddie-widdies," said Penelope Primrose, sitting down. There was no reply. Class Three were stuffing handkerchiefs into their mouths and trying not to laugh. Mr Majeika looked round the library, puzzled. Then he saw that

Penelope Primrose was sitting just beneath
a poster of herself, on which someone had
drawn a big beard and moustache.

"Hamish Bigmore –" began Mr Majeika.
But Penelope Primrose, not noticing that
anything was wrong, had begun her talk.

"Now, my little dearies," she was

saying, "I'm going to tell you all how my little bookie-wookies are made – these little bookie-wookies here." And she pointed at the display of her books on the table beside her.

At this, a roar of laughter broke out from Class Three. Mr Majeika looked at the books. Somebody had been altering the covers. The titles were supposed to be: *We All Love Little Bluebell*, *Little Bluebell Goes Shopping*, *Little Bluebell Meets the Firemen*, and *Little Bluebell in the Post Office*. Someone had used felt pens to change them to: *We All Hate Little Bluebell*, *Little Bluebell Goes Stark-raving Mad*, *Little Bluebell Meets Frankenstein*, and *Little Bluebell Gets Locked in the Loo*.

Penelope Primrose had seen the books, and was looking quite white in the face.

"Such *wicked* little tots!" she gasped. "I feel quite faint. I must have a sniff of these flowers to make myself better." She thrust her nose into the bunch of flowers in the vase in front of her – and then gave a shriek, because tucked in with the flowers were several large stinging-nettles.

"Hamish Bigmore!" roared Mr Majeika. "I know this is your doing!" Everyone looked round to see what Hamish would say. But he was nowhere to be seen. As Mr Majeika had shouted his name, there had been a flash of light, and Hamish had vanished.

"I didn't mean to make him disappear," said Mr Majeika, half an hour later, after Penelope Primrose had been soothed and sent away in a taxi (she said she would never go to another School Book Week again).

"You *never* mean to make him disappear, Mr Majeika," said Pete. "But it keeps happening."

This was true. During his first term at St Barty's, Mr Majeika had accidentally turned Hamish Bigmore into a frog. Another time, losing his temper with Hamish, he had sent him magically into a television set.

"I'll run and check the fish tank," said Jody, "just in case he's become a frog again. And Thomas, you turn on the TV and try that, just in case." But there were no frogs in the fish tank, and no sign of Hamish in the television programmes.

"He'll turn up," said Pete. "He always does, more's the pity. Let's get these books tidied away, Mr Majeika, and I'm sure he'll be back before the end of afternoon school."

"All right," said Mr Majeika, though he looked worried.

"I'll try and wipe the felt pen off the covers of Penelope Primrose's books," said

Thomas. "I wonder if Hamish has drawn things inside them too." He opened one of the books. "No, it looks all right – no felt-pen scribbles. Hey, wait a minute, what's this? I don't believe it. Come and see."

Class Three and Mr Majeika gathered round, and Thomas held up the book. It was *We All Love Little Bluebell*, and he had opened it at a page which had a picture of Little Bluebell talking to two other little rabbits. Except she wasn't just talking to two other little rabbits. She was talking to two other little rabbits and Hamish Bigmore.

"That's Hamish – I'd know him anywhere, even in a drawing by Penelope Primrose," said Thomas.

"Try the rest of the book," said Jody. "See if he's in any of the other pictures."

Thomas turned the pages. Sure enough, wherever there were pictures, Hamish was in them. He was dancing hand in hand through the woods with Bluebell and her rabbit friends, helping them to bake fairy-cakes, and putting up Christmas decorations in Little Bluebell's cottage. He looked absolutely furious at being there.

53

"Poor old Hamish," laughed Pete. "And what about the words? Let's see if he's got into them too."

He had. This is how *We All Love Little Bluebell* now began: "Once upon a time there was a pretty little rabbit called Little Bluebell. She lived in pretty little house in a pretty little wood, and she had three nice little friends called Little Snowdrop, Little Buttercup and Little Hamish."

"I bet he's loving every minute of it," giggled Thomas. "Do you think he's in the other Little Bluebell books too?"

He was. As they turned the pages, there was Little Hamish going shopping with Little Bluebell and the others, playing at fire-engines and postmen, and having a sweet little time.

"Do leave him there, Mr Majeika," said

Pete. "You can send his mum and dad the Little Bluebell books, and then they'll know he's safe."

"Oh, do, Mr Majeika," said Thomas. "Just for a few days." But Mr Majeika shook his head.

"I'll have to fetch him out," he said. "If I can."

He shut his eyes and muttered some words. The Little Bluebell books began to shake and shiver, and from their pages out stepped Hamish Bigmore. And after him skipped Little Bluebell, Little Snowdrop and Little Buttercup.

"Wow," gasped Hamish. "You'll never guess where I've been."

Little Buttercup tugged at his hand. "Little Hamish! Little Hamish!" she piped. "Come back to Bluebell Wood, because it's

time to have fairy-cakes for tea." She had a
voice rather like Penelope Primrose.

"Naff off," said Hamish.

"Are we going to have Little Bluebell
and her friends in Class Three?" asked
Jody. "Wouldn't they be happier in the
infants' class?"

"I'll try and get them back into the
books," said Mr Majeika. "Wait a minute –
what's going on?"

The other books on the library shelves were beginning to shake and shiver too, and other figures were starting to step from their pages. "Gosh," said Thomas, "isn't that Robin Hood?"

"And there's Toad, Mole, Rat and Badger," said Jody excitedly.

From some shelves at the back of the library, where science-fiction and fantasy

were stored, came Superman, Batman, and the strange creatures from *Star Wars*, while a nasty smell suggested that Fungus the Bogeyman couldn't be far away.

"Oh dear," said Mr Majeika, "I seem to have made the spell to release Hamish too strong."

Soon the library was packed with peculiar beings, creatures from outer space, and characters from comic books. There was the sound of breaking glass. "Watch it!" called Jody. "Hamish has teamed up with Dennis the Menace, and they've just smashed a window."

"It's fantastic, Mr Majeika," said Pete. "You ought to ring up the television people and the newspapers. Here's all these famous characters from the books, in real life."

"I know," said Mr Majeika doubtfully.
"But I think there's going to be trouble
pretty soon." Indeed, Captain Hook and
several of the pirates from *Peter Pan* were
already climbing out into the playground,
intent on some mischief. Mr Toad was
following them, chortling, "I spy motor

cars outside! Poop poop! Just let me get my hands on them."

"Ladies and gentlemen and, er, creatures," called out Mr Majeika, "it's been delightful seeing you all, but would you, please, now go back into your books?"

There was a general muttering at this, and then a shout of "No we won't!"

"You can't blame them," said Thomas. "It must be very boring, being in the same book year after year, and going through the same adventures every time someone reads it."

"Well, I can't help that," said Mr Majeika anxiously. "They've got to get back on the pages at once, otherwise there may be awful trouble."

At that moment, Mr Potter opened the

door of the library, peered inside at the strange collection of figures, and said, "Ah, Majeika, having a Parents' Morning, I see." He closed the door and went.

"It's lucky he didn't notice anything," said Pete. "If you can't persuade them to go back into the books, Mr Majeika, perhaps you can do it with a spell?"

"I'll try," said Mr Majeika, and shut his eyes.

"Poor things," said Thomas. "They haven't had much of a holiday. If they had any sense, they'd go back into different books."

Mr Majeika had begun to mutter to himself, and the room was growing dark and the books on the shelves were starting to shake again. But several of the book characters had heard Thomas. "What a good idea," called out Robin Hood. "Come on, Batman, why don't you and I do a swap?" And soon the library was loud with cries of "I'll have your book and you have mine," and "Get out of the way – it's my turn in this one," as two different characters fought to get into the same book.

At last it grew quiet, and the room became light again. Jody breathed a sigh of relief. "Well, that's all right then, Mr Majeika," she said.

Mr Majeika opened his eyes. "I hope so," he said.

"They've certainly all gone," said Pete. "But let's check everything's OK." He took one of the books off the shelf.

It was *Alice in Wonderland*, and he opened it at the page which ought to show

Alice talking to the White Rabbit. But
instead of the White Rabbit, the picture
showed one of the creatures from *Star Wars*.

"There's something wrong with the

words, too," said Jody, looking over Pete's shoulder. "Alice's name has disappeared, and it's all about robots and things."

"And look at this," said Thomas, taking another book off the shelf. "It's *Black Beauty*, but a whole lot of characters from the *Beano* annual have got into the words and pictures."

"This is dreadful," said Mr Majeika. "They've really all been very naughty. How am I ever going to get them back into the right books?"

"I shouldn't bother," said Pete. "I'd got bored with most of the books in the library, but if they've all been changed, I'll start at the beginning and read right through them again."

"Me too," said Jody. "It'll make them much more exciting."

"Book Week is supposed to make books seem more interesting, isn't it?" said Thomas. "Well, Mr Majeika, you've certainly done that!"

3. *Hello, Europe!*

"Bonjour, Monsieur Majeika," said Jody. *"Parlez-vous français?"*

Mr Majeika sighed and scratched his head. *"Oui, Jody,"* he said slowly, thinking very hard about the words. *"Je* speak – I mean, *je parle français*. Oh dear, what a difficult business it is teaching French."

This term, Class Three were having French lessons, to prepare for a day-trip to France. "I thought a wizard would find it easy to speak in a strange language, Mr Majeika," said Thomas.

"I can speak in *some* strange languages," said Mr Majeika. "See if you understand this: OLLEH, SAMOHT. NAC UOY DNATSREDNU EM WON?"

"Gosh," said Thomas. "What language is that, Mr Majeika?"

"Upsidedownese," said Mr Majeika. "It's spoken by Australian wizards. Maybe if I wrote it, you'd work out what it meant. It's much easier than French."

"I've got an idea," said Jody. "Why don't you cast a spell over the whole class, so that we can all speak French perfectly?"

Mr Majeika looked doubtful. "I could try," he said. "But you know how my spells keep going wrong." He waved his arms in the air, and muttered some strange words to himself. "Now try," he said. "Just speak normally, and see if it comes out in French."

Jody drew a deep breath, and said "Hello!" It didn't come out in French, but her voice had turned into a deep bass.

Hamish Bigmore roared with laughter. "You sound really stupid," he said. And this made everyone else laugh, because Hamish's voice had gone high and squeaky. When Thomas and Pete tried to talk, their voices had American accents. Everyone else in Class Three spoke in some strange way, too!

"Well, I did warn you," sighed Mr Majeika, and he waved his hands again and muttered some more words.

"Never mind," said Jody, relieved to find that her normal voice had come back. "We'll just have to work hard at learning French."

"What a waste of time," snarled Hamish. "Isn't it stupid of the French to speak a different language from us? I bet they all talk English really, when we're not there. They only *pretend* to have their own language, just to annoy us."

"Something tells me," said Pete, "that Hamish Bigmore is going to be an absolute pest on this French trip."

In fact, on the journey to France he behaved perfectly well. Or rather, no one noticed him being a nuisance. This was because so many odd things were happening on board Class Three's bus.

The fun started on the way to Dover, where they were supposed to catch a hovercraft to cross the Channel. The traffic had been very slow all the way from St Barty's, and now it had come to a complete standstill.

"Oh dear," said Mr Majeika, looking at his watch. "The hovercraft leaves in half an hour. I'm afraid we're going to miss it."

"Boo-hoo," wailed Melanie, bursting into tears, as she always did when anything went wrong.

"It's all right," said Mr Majeika, and he turned to the bus driver. "Have you got a good head for heights?" he asked him.

"You bet," said the driver. "I used to be the window cleaner for an office block."

"In that case," said Mr Majeika, "hold on tight, everybody, and up we go!"

He shut his eyes, waved his hands, muttered some words, and the bus began to rise into the air. Up, up, it went, until it was floating above the tops of all the lorries and cars that were jammed together below. The other drivers stared in

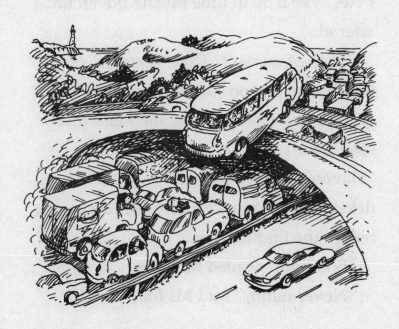

amazement as the bus began to fly over the traffic jam.

"Cor," said the driver, "this beats the telly, it does."

"I feel sick," sobbed Melanie, as the bus swayed up and down in the air. But everyone else was delighted.

"This is fantastic, Mr Majeika," said Pete. "We'll be in time for the hovercraft after all."

But they weren't. They floated down into the hoverport, and drove up to the gates, but a cross-looking man had just shut them. "Too late!" he shouted. "Haven't you read what it says on the tickets? Buses must be here half an hour before the flight leaves."

"Boo-hoo!" wailed Melanie.

"Never mind," said Mr Majeika. "I

expect we can manage it without a hovercraft. Do you get seasick?" he asked the bus driver.

"Not on your life," said the driver cheerfully. "Before I became a window cleaner I was in the Navy."

"Then up we go again," said Mr Majeika, and shut his eyes, waved his hands, and muttered some more words. The bus rose once more in the air, and in a few moments it was flying across the English Channel, high above the waves – and high above the hovercraft, which they could see churning its way towards France.

"'A life on the ocean wave,'" sang the driver, "'is the only life for me.'" He grinned at Mr Majeika. "This is better than the movies!"

"I'm going to be sick," snivelled

Melanie, but Mr Majeika gave her a magic seasickness pill, and she soon felt fine. After only a few minutes, the bus landed on the beach in France, just as the hovercraft was coming in.

"We had a much better journey than them," said Jody, pointing at the passengers, who were climbing off the hovercraft, looking very green in the face because the sea had been rough.

In a few moments, everyone's passports had been checked by the French officials, and they drove off into the town, where they were to spend the day. "We haven't got long," Mr Majeika explained to everyone, "so please will everybody behave themselves and stick with the class? I don't want anyone wandering off, so that we have to waste time finding them. The first thing we'll do is go and see some typical French shops. You can all practise the French you've been learning, because you'll find lots of nice things to buy."

They had all brought some French money – all except Hamish Bigmore. "The only real money is English money," he said. "They only have this French stuff to annoy us. And they'll take English money when I offer it to them, because they know it's better than French. You'll see!"

The bus parked in a square in the middle of the town, and everyone got out. "You can have fifteen minutes for shopping," called Mr Majeika. "There's a pastry shop with lots of nice cakes, a clothes shop which also sells toys, a newspaper shop which sells French comics, and a record

shop where you can buy French pop
music. Don't spend all your money at
once, because you may want to buy
something later. See you all back at the bus
in a quarter of an hour."

Jody, Thomas and Pete decided to go to
the record shop and see what French pop
music was like. They were a bit

disappointed, because most of the records, CDs and cassettes in the shop were by pop groups they'd heard before. So they tried the newspaper shop, but again the comics were ones they knew already, featuring characters like Astérix and Tintin. "This is boring," said Pete. "France seems just the same as England."

"It can't *all* be the same," said Jody. "My dad told me to try the pastry shops. He said they make wonderful cakes and chocolates that you never get in England."

"Sounds OK," said Thomas. "Come on."

There was trouble going on in the pastry shop. Two *gendarmes*, which is the French name for policemen, were dragging somebody out into the street. He was smeared all over with chocolate.

"It looks like Hamish Bigmore," said Pete.

The shopkeeper was waving his hands about angrily, and chattering away furiously in French. "Don't be silly," shouted Hamish at him. "I know you really speak English, so stop that jabbering."

The *gendarmes* were blowing their whistles angrily. They were about to hustle Hamish into a police car, when up rushed Mr Majeika. With great difficulty, he persuaded the shopkeeper and the *gendarmes* that he was Hamish's teacher, and he asked them what was wrong.

The shopkeeper said a great deal in French, very fast. Mr Majeika scratched his head. "Let me guess," he said to Hamish. "You bought a lot of chocolates and then

tried to pay for them with English money, and when they wouldn't take it, you ate the chocolates anyway. Is that true?"

"You bet it is," said Hamish, licking his lips.

"Well, you deserve to be taken to the police station, to teach you a lesson," said Mr Majeika. "But so as not to spoil our day-trip, I'll see what I can do." He waved his hands and muttered some words. "Now," he said, "if the shopkeeper looks on his counter, I think he'll find that all the chocolates that Hamish ate have reappeared."

It was true. The shopkeeper was quite astonished, and the *gendarmes* seemed cross that they couldn't arrest Hamish, but everyone soon calmed down and the *gendarmes* drove off in their police car.

"Now," said Mr Majeika, "as we've finished shopping, let's all go and have lunch. Then you can see what French food is like."

"I bet it's the same as English food," said Pete, "just like the pop records and the comics."

But it wasn't. There were some very

strange-sounding things on the menu, and they had to spend a long time puzzling over the names of the dishes, with the help of a dictionary. "Look at this!" cried Mr Majeika excitedly. "*Escargots* means 'snails'. They're serving snails for lunch! How wonderful – I haven't tasted snails since I was a wizard. They used to be my favourite food."

"It sounds horrid," said Jody, making a face. "But snails is a very famous French dish, Mr Majeika, so you ought to try it."

"Yuck," said Hamish Bigmore. "No poisonous French rubbish for me. I'll have beefburger and chips, with baked beans."

"It's not on the menu, Hamish," said Mr Majeika. "You'll have to eat something French."

"Well, I won't," said Hamish crossly, and got up. "I'm going to see if there's somewhere in this crummy town that serves decent food, like we have in England."

He stormed out of the restaurant, and for a while things were nice and peaceful. Mr Majeika's snails came, and he said they were delicious. Jody is a vegetarian, so she had mushroom soup and a nice dish made out of potatoes and cheese, and Thomas and Pete had steak with salad. They were all really enjoying themselves, when they heard police whistles blowing outside the restaurant.

"Oh dear," said Mr Majeika, "I hope it isn't Hamish."

Pete went and looked out of the window. "Yes it is," he said. "They're arresting him again."

Mr Majeika hurried outside. This time it took much longer to discover what Hamish had been doing, because it required a lot of long French words for the *gendarmes* to explain, and Mr Majeika had to keep using his dictionary. Hamish and the *gendarmes* were surrounded by a crowd of very cross old ladies, who were shaking their fists at Hamish, and chattering away

very fast in French.

"I think I understand," said Mr Majeika
at last. "It's all to do with bread."

"Bread?" said Jody, puzzled. "Hamish
doesn't like eating bread, does he?"

Mr Majeika shook his head. "He hasn't
been eating it. He's been breaking bits off

it. You see, French bread is sold in long sticks, called *baguettes*, and when people buy them they tuck them under their arms, or put them in their shopping bags so that the ends stick out, or if they're on bicycles they fasten them to the carrier at the back. And Hamish –"

"Don't tell me, let me guess," said Thomas. "Hamish has been going round the town, breaking off the ends of people's *baguettes*."

"That's right," said Mr Majeika gloomily. "Look!" The old ladies were all brandishing broken *baguettes*, with the ends chopped off them.

"Oh dear," said Jody, "do you think you can do something about it, Mr Majeika?"

"I'll have a try," said Mr Majeika. He shut his eyes, waved his hands, and muttered some words. Suddenly the old ladies stopped their chattering, and there were gasps of astonishment. The broken *baguettes* were suddenly unbroken again. The missing bits, which Hamish had knocked off, had been magically put back in place.

The *gendarmes* stared open-mouthed. Then they shrugged their shoulders, and let Hamish go. "You don't deserve to get away with this, Hamish," said Mr Majeika. "Now, everyone, before we go back to the bus, we're going to visit the cathedral. Come along, Hamish, and no more trouble-making."

"Cathedral," grumbled Hamish. "Who wants to see a stupid cathedral?" But he tagged along behind the rest of Class Three as they walked across the square and into the cathedral.

Inside it was very dark with the only light coming through stained-glass windows, making it difficult to see anything. Class Three and Mr Majeika looked around at the statues and candles. Then Jody said, "Hamish has vanished."

"Oh, bother," said Mr Majeika. "Where did he go?"

"Outside, I expect," said Pete. "He's probably gone to make some more trouble."

They all went outside, but there was no sign of Hamish.

"What a nuisance," said Mr Majeika. "We ought to be going home in a few minutes. I know, I'll put a spell on him to keep him in the same place, wherever he is. That means he won't be able to keep dodging away from us. All we have to do is look for him." He shut his eyes and waved his hands. "That should do it," he said. "Now, you all stay here, and I'll go and find him. While you're waiting, have a look at the stone carvings on the front of the cathedral. They're very interesting."

Off he went, and Thomas, Pete and Jody looked at the carvings. Strange creatures had been cut in the stone. They were meant to be devils and other monsters, and they were all very ugly. "That one's really dreadful," said Pete, pointing to a figure above one of the windows, which was baring its teeth at them.

"It's different from all the others," said Jody. "It reminds me of someone, but I can't think who."

"Can't you?" said Pete. "I can. It's just like Hamish Bigmore."

"Yes, isn't it?" said Thomas. "Isn't that odd? It means that hundreds of years ago, when they were building the cathedral and doing these carvings, there must have been somebody around who looked just like Hamish."

"I don't think so," said Jody. "I think Hamish must have climbed up that scaffolding, where they're mending the stonework, to do some mischief. And then Mr Majeika put the spell on him, and he's turned into a carving."

At that moment, Mr Majeika came back, looking worried. "I can't see

Hamish anywhere," he said.

"It's OK," said Pete, "we've found him." He pointed to the carving. "You can take the spell off him now, Mr Majeika."

"All right," said Mr Majeika, "I'll do my best." He thought for a moment, then muttered and waved his hands.

The carving of Hamish didn't move. "Perhaps it was the wrong spell," said Jody.

Mr Majeika shook his head. "I'm sure it wasn't," he said. "Perhaps I didn't say it loud enough, or perhaps –" He stopped, and a worried look appeared on his face. "Perhaps, as we're in France, I need to say the spell in French."

"But you managed to turn him into stone without speaking French," said Thomas.

"That spell used international magical words," explained Mr Majeika. "The one I was trying just now was in English. Come on, we're going to have to find a French magician."

They went off down the street, looking at the names above the shops. Suddenly Pete said: "Look – isn't that what we need?" He pointed at a small, dark shop, above which the sign said *Pierre Dubois, Magician*.

"Excellent!" cried Mr Majeika, pushing the shop door opened. But then he stopped and shook his head. Inside, the shop was full of conjuring tricks. There was a very ordinary-looking young man behind the counter. "This won't do," said Mr Majeika. "It's just a trick shop. What a pity."

"But look, Mr Majeika," said Jody, pointing at a half-open door which led into the room behind the shop. Through it, they could see a very old man, in a wizard's tall hat, sitting in a deep armchair. Asking the permission of the shopkeeper (as best they could in their broken French), Mr Majeika and the others pushed open the door. *"Bonjour,"* said Mr Majeika nervously to the old man, and then, "Why, it's my old chum from sorcery school, Daniel-Paul Lapin. How are you, Daniel-Paul?" He shook hands with the old French wizard, who smelt strongly of garlic, and quickly explained the problem.

"Ah, zat ees no problem," said Monsieur Lapin. "I will be, 'ow you say, de-lighted to come to zee cathedral and work zee spell in French. It ees a long time since I have done ze magic. I just sit here all ze day, watching my grandson sell ze conjuring tricks. Eet ees so boring! Spells are more, 'ow you say, fun!"

So off they all went to the cathedral, where Monsieur Lapin spoke a long spell in French. Hamish came to life at once, and climbed down the scaffolding, with a grin all over his face.

"Zere you are, my friend Majeika," said Monsieur Lapin. "I zink zat, next time you come to France, you 'ad better learn ze French."

"I think I had," said Mr Majeika. "But really, we've had far too many spells today. I'm sure I should stick to being an ordinary teacher, and not do any magic, or go looking for French wizards to do it for me. Don't you agree, everyone?"

No, they didn't agree at all.

Read more in Puffin

For complete information about books available from Puffin – and Penguin – and how to order them, contact us at the appropriate address below. Please note that for copyright reasons the selection of books varies from country to country.

www.puffin.co.uk

In the United Kingdom: Please write to Dept EP, Penguin Books Ltd,
Bath Road, Harmondsworth, West Drayton, Middlesex UB7 0DA

In the United States: Please write to Penguin Group (USA), Inc., P.O. Box 12289,
Dept B, Newark, New Jersey 07101–5289 or call 1–800–788–6262

In Canada: Please write to Penguin Books Canada Ltd,
10 Alcorn Avenue, Suite 300, Toronto, Ontario M4V 3B2

In Australia: Please write to Penguin Books Australia Ltd,
250 Camberwell Road, Camberwell, Victoria 3124

In New Zealand: Please write to Penguin Books (NZ) Ltd,
Private Bag 102902, North Shore Mail Centre, Auckland 10

In India: Please write to Penguin Books India Pvt Ltd,
11 Panscheel Shopping Centre, Panscheel Park, New Delhi 110 017

In the Netherlands: Please write to Penguin Books Netherlands bv,
Postbus 3507, NL–1001 AH Amsterdam

In Germany: Please write to Penguin Books Deutschland GmbH,
Metzlerstrasse 26, 60594 Frankfurt am Main

In Spain: Please write to Penguin Books S. A., Bravo Murillo 19,
1° B, 28015 Madrid

In Italy: Please write to Penguin Italia s.r.l.,
Via Felice Casati 20, I–20124 Milano

In France: Please write to Penguin France S. A.,
17 rue Lejeune, F–31000 Toulouse

In Japan: Please write to Penguin Books Japan, Ishikiribashi Building,
2–5–4, Suido, Bunkyo-ku, Tokyo 112

In South Africa: Please write to Longman Penguin Southern Africa (Pty) Ltd,
Private Bag X08, Bertsham 2013